THE CHRISTMAS SPIRIT

ISBN 978-1-64670-916-8 (Paperback)
ISBN 978-1-64670-917-5 (Digital)

Covenant Books, Inc.
11661 Hwy 707
Murrells Inlet, SC 29576
www.covenantbooks.com

THE CHRISTMAS SPIRIT

A Past-Your-Bedtime Story

Anthony Mazzone

The children cried out to see these Snowstars...

PART 1

In those days, in Deephaven, the day before Christmas had no eventide. The daylight would be gathered at the four corners of the earth and abruptly folded up like a sheet. As the frost came chilling in from the frozen North, the stars shone bright and bold, twinkling so hard that you could actually hear them jingle.

Almost everyone in the village, and of course all the dogs, came outside to watch. Not even woolen gloves could keep fingers from becoming icy cold. Wet noses too were cold. When faces turned to the stars, every breath became a cotton-like puff of air, a white cloud sailing off into the night.

This is how it used to be on the day before Christmas, in Deephaven, in the time of King Gregory Mustabeard, when there was black cold and aching darkness and bright golden stars. Those stars, as the night grew deeper, tinkled more loudly, twirled on their bottommost points. They twirled, each one, until exploding into great shiny crystalline shapes: not hexagons only but pentagons, tetrahedra, and fantastic dodecahedra, rosettes, and prisms, with each of their latticed plates sparkling in the night. The children cried out to see these snowstars, the dogs barked, and Beerbluff Thunderbelly bellowed. Thousands of shining snowstars fluttered to earth, leaving behind broad streaks in the black night sky

There made music too, melodies that broke into glassy crystals and floated down on the wind: distinct beads of sound chasing one another up and down the scales.

The snowstars fell for hours, singing as they came to rest, until, one by one, their melodies ceased. It was then that the Quiet closed upon the fields and houses, roads, and treetops. It was then that the fox in her den quieted her cubs; the snow bunting in the tree gentled her brood; the trees held their leaves close against the branches. Though the dogs knew not to bark, they could not stop their tails from whisking back and forth. All living things thrilled within. They all knew that the Quiet preceded the Christmas Spirit. She was on her way. In the silence, in the cold, in the almost painful upswing of gladness in the heart, they could feel her coming.

I am telling you this bedtime story, this past-your-bedtime story, so that you will know what the day before Christmas was like in those days. Remember, I'm speaking of the time before the Ill Wind and the Wolf at the Door, before Vitalian had crossed the Sands of Time to speak with the Tide and Old Man River, before he climbed Bifrost and heard the Music of the Spheres, even before he visited the dear Christmas Spirit herself, as told to do by the Northern Lights.

Now let me also tell a bit about Beerbluff Thunderbelly. No room was big enough for him. He was like a planet with his own gravitational field that drew all eyes toward him. Even his shadow in the starlight was fearsome. Farthest away was the dark shape of a hat made from wolf fur, then the lumpy outlines of the coat that covered his oblong chest and belly, hard like a huge block of ice. Then came flutters of thick branchy legs that merged in the blackness with his own enormous feet. Without those huge feet, he certainly could never have stood still, but would have toppled over time after time.

Beechcliff Thunder belly. 4 No room was big enough for him.

Vivian was happy to sit at the window of his cottage

Vitalian was happy to sit at the window of his cottage, for he loved just being in the same room as Mother and Father. Ever since he could remember, everything had been glad and familiar, from Father's bright gray-blue eyes to the tight bow of Mother's apron strings. And now the red-hot glow of burning coals was all about her as she opened the door of the oven, letting out steam and the delicious odor of gingerbread, bubbling and baking away. Across the room at the other window, impinging the space, Father held a stone tankard of steaming liquid in his hand. From time to time, he would put back the lid and raise it to his lips. With two fingers of the other hand, he lifted his brave mustache, and into his mouth went quantities of some gurgling liquid. The corners of his eyes crinkled up, and then with a happy sigh, he lowered the tankard and shut the lid. Again he laughed to himself, a tremor deep in some mountain, and you laughed also to see him so merry.

Mother's red-and-white checkered apron, the quilted upholstery of the armchairs, Father's eyes—all the colors seemed radiant and warm. Outside, the villagers were waiting for the stars to turn into lovely singing snowstars, just as they did every Christmas Eve.

Then suddenly, it began. A movement caught Vitalian's eye. One little star twirled and chirped sharply like a bird as Vitalian squirmed with delight. "They're starting to dance!" he cried across the room.

But no, the star did not dance or sing. Instead of twinkling louder, it dimmed quickly into blackness, as if its energy had been exhausted. Vitalian looked at the other stars strewn across the sky like toy jacks scattered by children at play. He knew each of them by name. Many a warm night he lay on his back in the fields near his home and longed for them. Beerbluff told him their names: red Antares and royal Rigel, eagle-like Altair, and Bellatrix. Every now and then, one of these would start to twinkle brightly, but then tremble for a moment before fading away. Left behind was a cold, dull, and most feeble light. What was wrong? Vitalian looked at his father, and the gray-blue twinkle in his eyes had also grown dull. The liquid in the tankard had stopped steaming. All over the village, people began to hurry indoors, leaving a cold draft to crawl through the empty streets. Thick wisps of something gray came drifting in from the North. The stars tried to back into their sky-holes. With his breath growing short, Vitalian watched the dirty wisps of cloud grow thicker. He wanted to cry when the wisps crept over his little stars one by one, covering them over and plugging up their holes. And horrible to see, it was not long before all the stars, even faithful Polaris, were covered with a suffocating blanket. Only Aldebaran, bravest of all, continued to shine brilliantly. The wisps of cloud circled and twisted about him, keeping just out of reach of his brassy points. Then gathering from all over like sticky wads of cotton, they advanced together. Aldebaran concentrated himself into a single one of his points, which, fierce and bright, stabbed out into the dirty clouds and scattered them in all directions. Stinking frayed shreds floated heavily down to earth. Once again the wisps thickened and closed around the star, and once again a sharp bright point bit into them. But Aldebaran gradually grew smaller, and each of his eight points blazed out in succession against the suffocating masses of cloud. Now Vitalian could see how beautiful Aldebaran was, as the golden light was concentrated into a single burning center. It was so bright that, etched against the dullness beyond, it almost punctured one's eyes. With a wild imagining, Vitalian hoped for a moment that perhaps the star would twinkle and explode, would become a snowstar and sing a joyful song, that the clouds would somehow grow thin and vapory and melt off the other stars too. But they banked into huge diseased clusters until Aldebaran, exhausted, lost his hold. He grew baggy and dull. The wisps of cloud crawled all over him like hairy spiders. For a few seconds, a golden ghost of a presence could be seen, and then Aldebaran was gone. The last of the stars was gone. Everyone took breath as if beneath a blanket. Only the wisps of cloud moved now, blowing about in the air, terrible and cruel.

Beerbluff Thunderbelly, the oldest and biggest man in the village, had no fear. Though his hair was white and hung to his shoulders, and though his beard was white and longer than his hair, Beerbluff was still strong and straight, with veins on his arms like knotty tree roots. He alone remained outdoors, bellowing at the sky. Father walked to the cabin door. Fixed into the thick oak was a broad iron bolt, which fitted into a ring upon the stone doorjamb. This was the first time that Vitalian had ever seen the bolt run home.

From far away there came a low drawn-out moan as if something monstrous were stirring, turning over in pain. Such a thin, lonely, evil sound: it seemed to go through your body and right into your heart.

The fire in the hearth flared up flickered out. The coals gave no heat. Shadows crept forth from the corners of the room. Mother took the bread out of the oven, and all the loaves were dry and flat.

"Let us go to bed," she said, hugging Vitalian.

"The Christmas Spirit will not come tonight," said Father in a whisper.

Mother took out some smelly woolen blankets. She had Vitalian dress in red pajamas and then with a quiet kiss sent him to his frozen bed. He had to bite his lips to keep from crying out, and he was shaking all over with cold and fright. And no matter how hard he tried to control his voice, it trembled when he asked, "Mother, what happened to Aldebaran? Why aren't the snowstars going to sing? Where is the Christmas Spirit this year?"

Before she could answer, there came a fierce howl. The wind gathered strength from high on the mountains and came exploding through the streets of the village. It roared and trumpeted; it howled and whooshed around doors and windows and tried to sneak inside wherever it could. Shutters were blown open and shattered to splinters against the stone walls. Chimneys were blown down into the streets where the red bricks lay scattered all over the cobblestones. Mothers held their children; fathers ran helplessly around the rooms. There was crying and wailing off in the distance. This was a wind that tore and bit and killed: it was the Ill Wind that blows nobody any good.

Meanwhile the darkness had congealed like a blood pudding set out to cool. Every house was dark and cold as the screaming Wind blustered about outside. For most of the night, Vitalian lay shivering beneath the scratchy blanket, listening to the maddened Ill Wind and trying not to notice the sour, sickly smell upon it.

"Who-o-o, wh-o, who-o-o!"

And shuddering, he imagined that this must be the breath of some loathsome monster belching its pollution upon the world.

In the midst of this nightmare, no one remembered that this was still Christmas Eve. The darksome hand of terror had come down from the mountains to lay its cold grip upon every heart, squeezing tighter until not a drop of courage was left. Still worse, the wolves were driven forth from the heights and down into the village. Their empty bellies were ravening for something to devour, and there came to Vitalian's ears a low "krr-rr, krr-rr-rr, krr-rr-rr" as the wolves trotted through the streets, one stopping and waiting before each door.

Never in his lifetime had the wolves made their appearance, but he had sometimes heard of them from Beerbluff. Vitalian often went to his workshop and stayed with him as he sawed, hammered, planed, fixed, and fitted. He would sit astride one of the great sawhorses, breathing the comforting scent of freshly planed wood. There among the wood shavings and sawdust, Beerbluff had often told Vitalian stories of the Old Days, including the Wolves at the Door.

"They are wondrously ugly," he told Vitalian, "rabid and wicked. Yet they are cowardly and stupid creatures. The Ill Wind sends them back and forth across the mountains, lashing them on wherever there is some hellish work to be done." It was said that Beerbluff had read many books in his youth and had seen much during his travels.

Vitalian often frightened himself by thinking of those lurking wolves. And once in a while, usually in the dead of a winter's night, a pain-filled animal howl could be heard from far off in the mountains. He would picture to himself the wolves' great teeth and lolling tongues, their coarse quivering bodies striped and spotted all over. And now he realized it was all for real. One of those murderous creatures was standing right outside his door! He shivered, for the Wolf was at his door, and its red eyes were burning.

"I want to go to sleep, I want to go to sleep," Vitalian kept repeating to himself as he shifted in his bed. It was once so warm and comfortable but was now so lumpy and cold. "Maybe it will be different in the morning. Daddy and Beerbluff will go out with their axes, and everything will get fixed. Maybe when the sun rises, the clouds will disappear and the Wolves will go running back to their lairs. Now I don't even want to hear the snowflakes singing, or to see the Christmas Spirit with her halo of rainbows, or hear her jingling bracelets. No, all I want is for everything to be again just like it was."

It was almost impossible to believe that the Wolf was actually at his door, that before dawn he, Vitalian, could well be torn apart and devoured. Yet the gravelly "Krr-rr, krr-rr-rr" came to his ears, and he understood that his life would eventually have to come to this, to some dread moment of pain and terror.

But Vitalian, frightened though he was, had to see the Wolf for himself. Though the putrid fog clung to everything, the Ill Wind had died down for a moment. It was colder than ever before. The soles of Vitalian's feet practically froze onto the stones of the floor when he got out of bed. He shivered violently as he dragged an old armchair to the bedroom window. Then, standing upon the faded cushion, he looked out into the night and for the first time saw the fierce Wolf at the Door. At first, all he noticed were two rows of yellow teeth, just made for crunching bones. As for what was behind them, he knew: what odorous breath, what a rough, slimy, sandpapery slab of a tongue, ugly as a piece of pickled meat, what rancid and noisome innards gorged with blood. He raised his clenched hands to his face, pressed his palms to his chin, and bit his fingers to keep from screaming.

There was a movement. A heavy head turned, and two reddish eyes glimmered. The Wolf pranced about on his fat paws, and yellow saliva dripped from his tongue and sizzled on the ice. Vitalian bit his fingers harder. Suddenly the monster reared back on its haunches and, opening its nostrils to the sky, let out a great howl that rose in a quivering wail that froze the blood and caused ice to crackle around every door and window. To Vitalian, it was the sound of all pain and cruelty finding voice at once. Yet beneath his fear was something else. It seemed as if he were being invited now to examine all those things his mother had always said were bad for him, as if he could now get away with doing those shameful secret things. Another howl snaked and twisted into silence. The Ill Wind picked up again, and Vitalian felt that what floated upon it was the opposite of what the Christmas Spirit brought with her when she came dancing into town, rainbows at her sandaled feet, a halo of ice crystals about her head.

In the whole battered, trembling, helpless village, no man was unafraid except old Beerbluff Thunderbelly, who was full of years. And Vitalian saw him now, alone in the narrow lane outside. His long white hair and beard were shining in the darkness, flowing in the Wind.

What could Beerbluff be doing outside on this abominable night, among those murdering Wolves? Nevertheless, Vitalian's heart leapt like a jackrabbit at the sight of him. Beerbluff walked into the baleful red gleam of the Wolf's wicked eyes. And wouldn't the double row of hard yellow teeth tear and crunch his old bones, too? Wouldn't that savage animal crush and chew the life right out of him?

But no, the Wolf lowered his heavy head, and Beerbluff's hand, blue-veined and old, was placed upon it as a kind of rough caress. At that moment, some weight seemed to pass from Vitalian's shoulders, and a loud exhalation of relief arose from the entire village. There was the rapid flapping of wings as birds darted back to their nests from wherever they had taken refuge. Several of the wisps of cloud were ripped to shreds, and the tatters were blown away by what seemed to be a fresh wind high in the heavens. Now

But no, the wolf lowered his heavy head.

the Wolves at the Doors did not seem so terrible, and the devilish red gleam in their eyes was only a sickly glint of hunger. Suddenly, like a returning memory, Vitalian could sense just the slightest hint of the approach of the Christmas Spirit.

And there old Beerbluff stood. For a moment, Vitalian thought that deep within the pupils of the old man's eyes, he could see brown fields furrowed under a warm foreign sun. But before he could be certain, old Beerbluff motioned for him to come outside. Vitalian pushed the armchair back in its place and rushed to put slippers on his feet and a fur coat around his shoulders. At the front door, he had to stand on tiptoe in order to draw the broad iron bolt from the metal ring. It slipped back as softly as if it had been made of felt. He stepped out, gently closed the door behind, and the cold struck him like a slap in the face. Then right there in front of him, its head hanging low, the tail slowly waving from side to side, was the Wolf at his Door.

"You can touch him," Beerbluff said, almost impatiently.

Of course Vitalian had no wish to do such a thing, especially when he saw how thick and matter the fur was. But he stretched out his hand and ran it along the bony back, feeling the prickly barbs in each hair. The animal twisted about, lolled out it tongue.

"The time has come at last," said Beerbluff. "We have gained a respite— an interlude. But now your time has come. Your journey, like mine many years ago, must begin in the face of this Ill Wind that blows nobody any good."

Vitalian scarcely heard these words. He was thinking that he had somehow known all along that the stars, the rainbows, the snowstars held a special meaning for him alone. He was not really surprised to find himself out on this night. He knew somehow that all that was simple and familiar would have to be left behind forever. Beerbluff's wrinkled hand was heavy on his shoulder as they went through the village. Dull hungry animal eyes peered at them from the doorways.

Beerbluff spoke: "The battle has shifted, and our Assailant has changed his ways." They passed now beyond the last houses of the town. "He is not a great venomous snake but a miserable worm that twists its way into men's hearts. Our Christmas Spirit knows that the people are still simple and good. But they take what is given as if it is due to them. Alas, Vitalian, it is not their due. The Christmas Spirit can no longer be so lavish her affections. She is the Christmas Child's gift and may only be given to those strong enough to desire her."

By no means did Vitalian understand what Beerbluff was saying. He was shivering with cold, and in any case he did not care greatly for all these words; he would just do what Beerbluff asked.

Up into the hills they went, the Ill Wind whipping and lashing at them, screaming terrible curses into their ears. Just when the Wind seemed to be turning them around, Vitalian felt as if he had woken from a dream.

Where am I going? he wondered. *This is me, little Vitalian, who has left home, climbing the hills at night, traveling to the North.*

Now they reached the top of the large hill just outside the village. The two stood for a moment to wipe the tears from their eyes, and Vitalian turned to look back in the direction from which they had come. Far below, the houses were nestled in the valley, clustered together for protection. In the midst of them was the sloping snow-covered roof of his own dear home, under which his two tired parents were sleeping. The thought brought tears to his eyes, and they were even harder to keep back when old Beerbluff placed an arm about his shoulders.

"It's a little cold," Vitalian blubbered, "and it makes my eyes water." But really he was shedding tears because his house seemed so tiny and helpless, because his parents were getting older every day, and because this was a forlorn, horrifying Christmas Eve.

Beerbluff turned him around to face the North. In the distance was an unbending line of dark trees. Perhaps there was no Wind stirring there.

Beyond the trees were the mountains, and high over all the smelly gray clouds were swishing and whirling.

"Go straight north," said Beerbluff, "and don't be afraid. Go forth to seek the Christmas Spirit. Find her, speak to her, and bring her back to us. I will comfort your mother and father. They also knew that this moment must come. Now go!"

The wind swept around Vitalian as he stood and watched Beerbluff go back down toward the village. And now all that could be seen was his enormous bulk, the shadows of his hat, his oblong chest, thick legs, and great feet stretching across the snow. Vitalian stood straight against the Wind. Then trusting to his slippered feet, and with a strong loud laugh, he bounded down the hill. Northward.

PART 2

The Ill Wind had altered everything: Vitalian would cross a whole plateau in two steps, but then it needed much walking to bring him to a boulder only a few feet away. Gravity pulled him up along the steepest slopes, then every bit of strength was required to clamber down into a valley.

So Vitalian struggled on until he left the hills and snow behind and came into a field of furze stretching toward a vast double row of trees. These were tall and leafy, equally spaced east and west, and all the same in girth. After entering under their branches, it was long before he reached their trunks. When he emerged from beneath the branches on the other side, he found himself under a starless night sky that was incredibly and intricately marbled with greenish veins of light.

The sky brightened until a hard green sun burst through the horizon as if it were a slippery glass ball that had been squeezed between a giant's fingers. It bounced once or twice in the air, then gleamed steadily down through its own luminescence: diaphanous celadon mists spiked with hard green rays above the yellow desert of the Sands of Time. The light was not diffused in the air but remained in beams as from a searchlight, focused downward in thick rays here and there upon the Sands. It was light without heat but whose substance you could feel with your hand. Vitalian reached out to touch one of those beams and was surprised to find it so cool. Then raising his eyes, he caught his breath.

Boundless and bare, the sand stretched like powdered gold toward the Ends of the Earth. There were soft piled mounds and gently rounded hillocks. Right through the sand coursed the blue ribbon of a river, which, smooth and clear, curved broadly and gracefully toward the foothills in the distance.

"The Sands of Time and the home of Old Man River," whispered Vitalian to himself. He recalled that when Thunderbelly had spoken of these things; his face was like that of a man in a dream. There was no Ill Wind blowing here.

Vitalian walked across the yellow Sands of Time for what seemed like days. Here and there the surface of the river was broken by the popping of white-tipped bubbles, as if living creatures were frolicking right below. It was the deepest, most cerulean, bubbly water he had ever seen, coursing through the burnished sand until it was lost in the deep sepia hills on the far horizon. Through yellow and blue riots of color, he trod toward this horizon, whistling and breaking into song as he walked through the shafts of green light falling about him like waterless rain:

> My steps are weary
> My heart is heavy
> She is gone,
> And I'll walk on!

He did not know why he was singing this song now, and as he sang, he noticed that the Sands were here and there piled into huge but strangely shaped dunes, no longer soft and rounded.

> My head held high, my spirits low
> Through the bitter world I go
> But she is gone
> And I'll walk on!

Suddenly one of the dunes shook violently. The sand hissed, and from it arose a strange figure. It was a grotesque, misshapen image of a man the color of burnt umber, and from every part of him the sand flowed down in a constant shifting stream.

Vitalian ran to help. "I'll have you out in a minute!" he cried, very frightened. "I'm so sorry, I didn't know you were buried here." He dug frantically, yet every handful he scooped away was immediately replaced by more sand. This was nothing less than the figure itself disintegrating into formless grains.

There was a gravelly laughter in the air. "You can't unbury me. I am among the Forgotten in the Sands of Time."

In fact, Vitalian could feel no flesh or muscle in him, but only a rough clod-like substance that crumbled at his touch into granular bits.

"No one can help me," continued the Sandman in a voice that was like the dry sibilation of a million gritty grains sliding to the earth. Vitalian himself was covered with a fine layer of sand; it scratched his eyes and gagged his throat. His blood ran cold when he ground it between his teeth.

"I've been here for many years, and there are many, many yet to come. No one knows what it is like to wait so long, so long for remembrance." The figure was rapidly disintegrating, yet a surprising gurgling sound came from deep within it. Two drops of water found their way out of two hollows, which were the Sandman's eyes, and they formed streaks of mud down what appeared to be his cheeks.

"I'm waiting, still waiting, and I'll wait until the mountains are washed away by the rain, until the rocks melt into sand. If these should melt, why not the hearts of men?" The streaks of mud became thick and shiny.

Vitalian's own eyes answered with tears. "Who are you, sir, and what is your name? I will remember you to the Christmas Spirit if I can find her."

The voice was so choked and cracked, so obscured by the sliding sand, that Vitalian could barely make out the words: "I am the Forgotten. No one remembers who I am. I am the Forgotten, and no one knows my name." The words came rapidly now, as only the bare hint of a shape could be discerned in the mounting pile of sand. "I too was once in the world, and you have seen me. You saw me in dirty clothes, wet with rain, and you were afraid of my mad red eyes and sad stare. You saw me about the most wretched and abandoned parts of the village, and you shuddered at the sight of my dirty hands and skinny limbs. At Christmas I walked the snowy streets all night long and listened to the laughter from within the homes. Every door was closed, for no one knew my name:

> A note of parting sorrow
> To reach an outstretched hand
> Slipped through the groping fingers
> Of this faceless man…

Then there was silence and no shape of a man. There was only a conical sandy mound, which sifted dryly through Vitalian's fingers.

"I will remember," said the boy softly, "I will remember, and I promise that you will not remain forever among the Forgotten. When I find the Christmas Spirit, she will come to set you free from the Sands of Time."

In answer, there arose a muffled sighing or moaning. As Vitalian made his way past the sand dunes along the river's edge, there came from them a grinding chorus of gravelly voices that tugged at his heart. These wretched lamentations made him weep, pursued him deep into the Sands until the moanings were intermingled with the noisy frothing of the river itself.

The rushing water lent a translucent blue tinge to the air above, and even to the bright green sunbeams. Vitalian was refreshed by a wonderful, wet clean scent in the air; he rounded bend after bend along the sluicing river. The bubbling and frothing and rushing reached a crescendo and then Vitalian saw him: the Old Man River.

There he was, all made of flowing water, lying comfortably in the riverbed. Gigantic and glinting in the green rays of the sun, his thin wavy fingers and long liquid legs curved off down the stream into the distance beyond. His whole body undulated softly, its outlines gradually fading away, blending into the river. Yes, one could say in fact that he *was* the river—all of it and all of him. His only clothes were long trailers and tendrils of vegetation, through which little fish of pristine pink and gold swam contentedly. Huge crabs made their homes in his beard, which, like his hair, was creamy white and floated all about to become the foam that crowned the crests of the ripples and flecked the rapids. At times, when his outline became so blurry and all of him so billowy and wavy that you could hardly make him out, you thought he might be a wonderful illusion. At other times, he lay more calmly in his bed, with an exhilarating odor coming from him, a pale blue aura all about, and above him a sprinkle of fine spray shot through with the beams of the verdant sun. You knew the Old Man River was for real when you saw the fantastic and short-lived rainbows created in the mist, rainbows of such bold shapes and shades of azure as can be seen nowhere else in the world.

Old Man River was indeed old and had been flowing like this almost since the beginning of time. Vitalian waded into the water and laughed as it gurgled and foamed about his legs. He came near a floating strand of hair and laid hold if it tightly with both hands, Then, delighted by the foamy babbling of the water, he splashed up onto the billowy chest, where, planted safely among the strands of Old Man River's beard, he called out with all his might.

Vitalian's little voice could scarcely be heard above the sighing and gushing of the playful waters. Again he called, and again, until Old Man River slowly lifted his head and tried to focus his pale blue eyes upon the strange creature standing in his beard among the crabs. The pupils expanded, and blue water tinted with green swished around in the eyeballs. Even there tiny fish were swimming about.

"Old Man River," the little boy yelled again, and Old Man River gurgled in surprise, spraying forth fine showers of water.

"Gurgle, gulp, trickle, drip," went Old Man River in a voice like colorful sea stones when they are rolled together on the floor of the river. "Gurgle, gulp, trickle, and what, bubble, can I do for you today, my funny droplet?" And he turned upon Vitalian a wavy, flowing smile. A lazy tenderness beamed forth from every frothy drop in his body, and the pale blue water in his eyeballs plashed about here and there. It was like looking through the porthole of a ship.

"I'm glad to be speaking to you," answered Vitalian politely. "You see, I'm trying to find the Christmas Spirit. And since you flow through so many distant lands, Old Man River, I thought you might be able to tell me where she is."

At mention of the Christmas Spirit, Old Man River's mouth dropped open, and out swam a fish almost as big as Vitalian himself. "Ah, the dear, dribble, little, droplet! Tell her I send many, many wet kisses. It's, gurgle, been, gulp, many a year since her tiny feet have splashed about in me." Then began such a symphony of gargles and gurgles, trickles, and dribbles that the words were completely washed away.

Vitalian persisted, "You don't understand, Old Man River, but this is Christmas Eve, and the stars have all been covered over with wisps of cloud, and I must bring the Christmas Spirit back, says Beerbluff Thunderbelly, for one last time."

At Beerbluff's name, Old Man River's mouth again dropped open, pouring forth another soaking torrent of water. "Sputter, see thou the Tide, little seeker. See thou, sputter, the Tide in the dry mountain hollow."

With an enormous gulp, Old Man River settled back contentedly into his bed. Vitalian turned his eyes to the craggy mountains above.

"Very old, very wise is the Tide," came a voice like waves lapping against the shore. "Very silent, trickle, very strong."

Vitalian plunged through soaking cataracts of water and waded up toward the mountains. The river gushed through narrow gorges; it plunged in cascades from rugged ledges and poured in billows over rocky precipices.

Vitalian could feel the water coursing around him, yet his pajamas gradually dried, and though splashed continuously, he found he was no longer wet at all. The farther he went, the paler grew the water, until it could not be seen at all. It was inaudible, invisible, dry, and he knew it existed only from the way it dragged against his legs. Everything grew pale, paler than the mist over the sea at dawn, than the transparent silver in the wings of morning—and as he approached the cavernous mountain hollow, nothing at all was visible. But Vitalian was not blind, for he could still see somehow; it was deep in his mind, and it was with his feelings.

It seemed he had entered some kind of huge empty space. He had the sense of cool vaults, arches, and enormously distant high-ceilinged domes. There was no air, no water, no color, no sound, but only the mind and something that tugged at it.

A tingling sensation ran through him like an electric charge. Cradled inside everything was a sort of slow throbbing, a recurring rise and fall, a slow, ceaseless ebb and flow. In the midst of this, he became aware of a rhythmical series of impulses, which he interpreted somewhere as words:

> Ebb and flow, come and go
> Side to side, far and wide
> Fast and slow, high and low
> Tide, the Tide, the Tide.

And an answering rhythm was in Vitalian himself, as if he too were a pulse, a force making known its desire to find the Christmas Spirit.

The pressure increased within the vacuum, the rhythm tightened. Beneath the ceaseless ebb and flow were little balanced cycles, and these too were composed of various repeated pulsations, each of which Vitalian followed with patient sympathy. Then he deliberately drew back and marveled at how harmoniously interlocked and interdependent were the cadences of the Tide, at how clear, simple, and grand was its design. In union with them, all did Vitalian breathe, and with them all did his spirit rise and fall as if it had been doing so forever.

There was a disturbance. The high-reaching vaults and arches contracted swiftly, and the rhythm was compressed intensely about Vitalian's senses. He felt that the whole universe had all of a sudden been drawn into a compact mass. Then it blew apart. Great chunks of matter, whole stars and planets, accelerated amid swirling clouds of cosmic dust through endless empty spaces. There were galactic pinwheels beating violently, and stars blinking with bright yellow or red lights, huge ringed planets throbbing as with pain, and moon-encircled planets that thrilled alternately with green and brown. Vitalian saw one planet more closely than the others. Wide beautiful land masses were upon it, and these too heaved heavily up and down. He saw a great tremor and an excruciating vibration as the tremor broke to the surface. It breached a hole, and from this streamed countless creature of every sort. Among them were men. Everything now was in turmoil: the heaving of the lands was violent and unbalanced, the galaxies tumbled ferociously, the rhythms ran together.

During the many ages, this endured Vitalian suffered greatly. But then in the breast of one of the men who had emerged from the breach in the earth was a heart that contracted and expanded also, that beat with strength and steadiness. One by one and slowly, the hearts of the other men began to beat along with it. Then with these hearts was gradually unified the heaving of the earth and the wheeling course of the planets. The galaxies, too, swing into line, and as the ages rolled, the universe's ebb and flow hummed in harmony with the one man's heart. At the end everything shuddered together in a single great chord; it had all become one vast, beating, ever-living heart.

A light beamed in the distance. Vitalian did not approach it, but it came swiftly upon him as if a dark tunnel were pulled away from all around. He shivered, and the vision of the great heart left his mind. His eyes perceived what could have been some kind of rainbow not far away. A part of him, however, heard the echo of the words:

> Still I hide, still I hide
> Near and far, far and wide
> Tide, the Tide, the Tide.

The boy knew now that he was out of the Tide. He was happier now than he had ever been. It was as if he had expanded with the universe and was now a bottomless hole into which a wild joy was poured. Such joy would have been too much for the boy who had first entered the Tide. But this was a new Vitalian, free from all that was small and cold. His pajamas draped themselves about him like the raiment of a king.

He wondered neither at the lights above nor at the gleaming porphyry rocks beneath his feet. He could not wonder or think, he could only hear: music as if made by hidden instruments of spun gold, notes honeyed and smooth and exhaled from each atom of air, streamed from every gradation of color. There were harmonies inside him, melodies outside, contrapuntal chimes in every space: the Music of the Spheres.

Vitalian, soul filled with melody, lifted his eyes. Before him shimmered a great gabled bridge where emerald green and complected gold, the deepest blues and red, purples, and pinks wove themselves into a vast geometrical arabesque. It was the bridge of Bifrost, reaching right to the throne of the fabulous Northern Lights.

At the foot of Bifrost waved a lone flower. Try as he would to focus his sight upon it, he could not. It was somehow like seeing every flower that ever was: every dahlia and daisy, begonia and zinnia, celandine and blossoming eglantine. And it was really one color yet every color in the world. He caressed the flower's downy stem, rubbed the gold dust on the petals. Then those petals parted, and from somewhere came a musical voice piping above the Music of the Spheres—not frail and thin as might be expected from a flower, but full-voiced and rounded.

'I must bloom, and will bloom'

"I must bloom and will bloom," sang the flower. Each word was a different tone, and all were voiced together as a single chord. "I will bloom and I must bloom, for I am the Amaranth that never fades. You must also bloom: in the chilling wind, in the choking dust, beneath the destructive storm. Bloom for the Heart that loves you and for His Christmas Spirit." Vitalian looked at her with dew in his eyes. He would bloom, in spite of the Ill Wind and the Wolf at the Door. Yes, even in spite of the innocent chimneys that lay broken and whose bricks were strewn about the village streets. He had to bloom, even when called far away from home to seek a Spirit he had only spoken to in his heart.

When Vitalian stepped onto Bifrost to begin his climb to the Northern Lights, perfume as of honeysuckle filled his senses. The Amaranth leaned over for a last caress, and little pointy-eared elves with sharp hats ran down the bridge to welcome him. They were so quick that Vitalian could only catch glimpses of tiny legs and green bodies, of pointy ears and hats. They never stopped chattering to one another, though they addressed not a sound to him. Their voices remained constantly on a single pitch. They escorted him higher and higher on the rainbow bridge, and now the perfume was like some a combination of oleander, lontana, and lavender; there were hints of sweet jasmine and dulcet cinnamon, the pungency of marjoram, the redolence of primrose, immortelles, and balmy mimosa.

The elves ran about, and their chattering voices went completely through Vitalian. Sometimes the Music of the Spheres sounded rose or mauve; at other times it was blue. The perfume, too, could be loud or soft. When Vitalian passed through the clouds, their silver linings shivered like tinsel. His mouth watered at the metallic taste it brought to the tip of his tongue, and his body tingled all the way down to his feet. As he approached the sky, Bifrost glazed into pearl. Far below was the silent Tide and the lovely Amaranth, and somewhere else was an emerald green sun beaming upon an infinity of shining yellow sand washed by Old Man River.

Then he was through the sky, gazing upon its surface, which looked like glossy pearl touched with pallid gleams of silver. Here and there in the distance were holes stuffed from below with ragged gray clouds.

Higher went Vitalian toward the polished throne of the Northern Lights. And as he approached, the continuous melody of the Music of the Spheres, along with the scintillating rainbow of color, rose to a climax in one single complex array of splendor. The elves chattered, then scattered away, and Vitalian felt as if he had always known and had always been meant to be a part of this vast and logical glory. Below were the shifting chromatic complications of Bifrost, sweeping down until lost in the silver linings of the clouds. Above rose the powerful Northern Lights upon his polished crystal throne. He was so huge that the heavens, fretted with fiery streaks of mauve and vermillion, scarcely seemed able to contain him. Long golden rays were streaming down from the zenith above and fell right upon his baldric, which was made of burnished bronze and reflected the golden rays in all directions. The Northern Lights' forehead was vast and furrowed, his head surrounded with a halo of shimmering gold.

"Come closer. Fear not."

"Come closer. Fear not," Vitalian felt the gentle voice. He had never felt so comfortable, so wholly at home as he did upon hearing those words. "What you need has already been purchased for you. Now come, you are at home. What is it you wish?"

Vitalian, enveloped by the reflected light, answered in his heart: "I want to find the Christmas Spirit, because at home it is Christmas Eve and she has not come to us. All the doors are locked, and everyone is hiding from the Ill Wind and the Wolves at the Door."

"And you've come here to speak to her for them?" The heavens darkened almost imperceptibly to a russet glow spiraled with streaks of variegated gold.

"I have, because Beerbluff Thunderbelly asked me to. But can you please tell me where to find her? I miss Mother and Father. They will soon wake up, and I would not want them to find me gone."

The Northern Lights inclined his great head and motioned for Vitalian to enter into the mist beneath his throne. "In the raining mist below, child, you will find the Christmas Spirit." The reflected light from the baldric of the Northern Lights set Vitalian's heart to ringing as if it were full of Christmas bells.

Beneath the throne was a frosty, silvery mist. Here and there in the mist fantastic ice crystals floated about, and under his slippers the snow sparkled as if it had been strewn with diamonds. Then there came to his eyes—his real eyes—a most beautiful sight. In the mist ahead was a young girl sitting upon a mound of pure white snow. Her elbows rested on her lap, and her chin was in her hands. She wore a simple white gown gathered at the waist by a thin gold band. Bright gold, too, were the sandals on her feet, and golden was the hair flowing down on her shoulders. Sparkling ice crystals, like alabaster barely tinged with blue, hung from the gentle curves of her ears. Bracelets of the same encircled her wrist. Her big aquamarine eyes refreshed Vitalian like pools of clean water.

A bud in Vitalian's soul bloomed. He thought he would die of happiness when she raised her head, brushed aside a lock of golden hair, and looked at him. Tears stood in her eyes—blue as the summer sky in the afternoon—as welling from a mountain spring. Vitalian came forward and put his arms around her. He felt as if his arms had always been empty and had always ached to shelter her. He had no doubt that this was the Christmas Spirit herself, the object of his search, for whom he had endured the fear and loneliness. He wondered that this delicate girl should be the spirit of such tremendous and powerful joy, but he heard again those words of Beerbluff: "You cannot despise as little that without which the great cannot come to pass."

"Deephaven is waiting for you, dear Christmas Spirit. We are waiting for you still."

When she spoke, her voice echoed like a violin inside him: "But you have not prepared a place."

"And our hearts ache terribly, too, dear Christmas Spirit. We are lonely and wait for you still. You came not, and we are afraid.

Upon a mound of pure white snow

In the mist ahead was a young girl sitting

32

Vitalian bathed in the depths of those eyes. Then the coolness seemed to recede to the fringes of the rayed irises, and within that pure blue, Vitalian saw several figures. One was a woman of great beauty, gentle and noble. Noble and princely also was the man kneeling beside her. They gazed with love and awe at the Christmas Child lying in the straw before them. Vitalian could hear the reassuring beat of a heart. There was tranquility and peace there, and boundless power too. Yet he who had passed through the Tide could feel also a bottomless sympathy, a measureless apprehensive sorrow. Vitalian strained to catch a glimpse of the Child. Leaning forward, he found himself again looking right into two tranquil blue pools and was aware once more of the Christmas Spirit.

She spoke: "The Child is the Heart who gathers to himself all poor, simple, and ragged things. But in the village, too many of the poor have become ashamed, and the simple have grown cold. They will not be gathered. Now the joy I bring cannot be purchased, cannot be held in arms that are already full of other things. The poor have no joy for the joyful have no poverty. I bring His gifts with me, yet they think I can be brought with gifts."

The Northern Lights penetrated even here through the mist, lending a gilded glow to the random ice crystals. The Christmas Child was close by, Vitalian knew. He had never stopped feeling Him since passing through the Tide, had continually heard Him somewhere in the Music of the Spheres, had practically seen Him beyond the Northern Lights.

"Can we love being poor when there are Wolves at our doors? Or dwell in peace where the Ill Wind blows?" Vitalian's voice was very sad. He was, after all, a little boy far away from home.

The Christmas Spirit looked at him with eyes that would engulf him in gentleness: "Oh, if you asked, He would change the Wind into a harmless puff of air! And the Wolves in a minute would wag their tails like little puppies!" She laughed now. "And I, too, would fill everyone's heart with singing for Him, and I would dance into town amid a shower of winter rainbows."

"Then why won't you visit us and set us to singing at least one last time? Not everyone has forgotten. Old Beerbluff, who sent me here, is very old and good. And last winter, when I was sick, Mother and Father spent all they had to make me well again. Come back to us, Christmas Spirit, come, for there are many who love you still."

The Christmas Spirit's laughter exhilarated him. Her blue eyes sparkled as she said, "As for you, yes, I know the secret joy that sometimes fills your heart at night. I know how quickly tears sneak into your eyes when you look in on Mother and Father holding hands before the fire. I remember one time, in the dead of a cold winter, when you saved your fresh bread from dinner in order to feed one poor hungry man, and the crumbs you scattered for the needful birds. You smiled later and felt warm all over when your stomach growled as you lay in bed."

graceful little

snow buntings, weren't they?

"I've forgotten all about that—yes, they were graceful little snow buntings, weren't they? And they had white-tipped wings."

Then the Christmas Spirit stood. Her eyes danced. "And now you're here, and very much in love with me." A brilliant smile was on her lips.

Something squirmed about inside Vitalian's chest, until from the delicately sculpted frame of the Christmas Spirit there flowed a warm power. Her thick golden tresses streamed down upon the whiteness of her gown. In the swirling mist, the happiness charged its way through him. He felt like jumping about, or loudly singing some crazy song. It's even possible he'd have used Bifrost as a sliding board, or tweaked the Northern Lights' nose if the Christmas Spirit had asked him to.

"Now come with me, for it seems I may yet dance once more in your world."

But as Vitalian only gazed at her with open mouth, stared at the condensed crystals sparkling on her eyelashes, she took him by the hand. Even as they made their way over the crunching snow beneath the throne of the Northern Lights, Vitalian was aware only of that hand in his, and of his arm tingling all the way to the shoulder, and of his heart jingling in tune with the blue-hearted earrings.

When they came out of the mist, the Christmas Spirit seemed larger than before. Indeed, Vitalian wondered how he could have ever thought of her as almost a child. His heart hammered whenever her earrings and bracelets tinkled. What was happening, he wondered briefly. Had he actually found and loved the Christmas Spirit herself?

They stood before the great crystal throne. It was polished to a translucent pearly glow, and the sheen in the heavens was a multicolored gloriole with outlines leafed in gold. Even the nimbus encircling the Northern Lights seemed somehow richer than before. Of course the Christmas Spirit was impossibly beautiful, and poor Vitalian fell more impossibly in love with her.

It was with deep-voiced kindness the Northern Lights addressed them: "Daughter of delight and dearest child of earth, both of you, come close and tell me what you wish."

In the same tranquil way, the Christmas Spirit answered, "We ask that you extend your canopy of light over Deephaven, that it may accompany us once more on the way."

A furrowed brow framed by a waving mane of illuminated hair inclined slightly forward in the lofty distances above.

The Christmas Spirit continued, "We do not hold the field any longer, but at least somewhere I am remembered. I've been told that many of the gentle stand fast. Yes, I was told so by this little one"—she squeezed Vitalian's hand—"who opened his heart and sought me alone in the untrodden ways. Kindness started in his loving heart, and for this I wish to make the hearts of everyone sing with joy!"

Vitalian saw the mane of hair and the noble head far above, then heard the healing words: "Then go once more, and my Lights will go with you. Bring joy to the steadfast and relief to the poor. May the kind flowers of His love spring up to soften your way."

From on high a brilliant opalescence spread through the heavens. There was an opening toward the zenith, and out poured a brilliant flood of light comprised of three distinct beams. It fell full upon the Northern Lights' burnished baldric and was reflected toward Vitalian and the Christmas Spirit. I can't say what happened to them at that point. Only know that they were transformed into something greater.

PART 3

I f every atom in the universe were a fine-tuned instrument, and if these all swelled together in rhapsodic harmony, only then could anything have equaled the transcendent beauty of the Music of the Spheres. When the pair turned and set out on Bifrost, they did not need to walk. They flew along as blazing streaks of prismatic light spun away beneath their feet. As they passed, the colors behind hissed and sparkled, coming close to being alive.

38

In no time at all, they had passed through the bright floor of the sky and penetrated the silver linings of the clouds. The elves leaped with delirious joy at the sight. Vitalian found he could now clearly see each one of their red-cheeked chubby faces and count their nimble, clean-cut limbs. Never slowing down, he reached out and gathered up a squirming armful of tiny bodies. With hats all askew, the elves laughed and chattered together, their voices like hollow reeds in his soul, and they kissed him a thousand times. But the Christmas Spirit again grasped Vitalian's hand, and she whisked him still downward amid the wild fragrances and through the solid green beams of the sun. Down they went to the mountains in which the iridescent Amaranth had her quiet abode. She turned her flowered head as the two approached, her downy leaves waving gracefully with each varicolored petal unfolding in welcome. They came to rest, and the petals exploded into a volcano of color: screaming yellows burst open to pour forth streams of blue; there were blacks deep enough to draw your eyes down into them and whites so bright you could feel them upon your skin. The multiform leaves flooded with green, orange, red, and gold—or rather there were such colors in the shape of leaves.

With his hands running all over the silky blues and hard reds, and with his fingers sinking into spongy ambers, Vitalian cried out, "Amaranth, you are so beautiful it will surely make me happy forever! Every flower in the unseen meadows of people's hearts, every good work blossoming on the earth is revealed in you. How can this be? What is it that makes you so?"

In answer, the Amaranth grew so dazzling she would have erupted into flame if not for the elegant cooling presence of the Christmas Spirit. Straight and shapely, she was standing with clear blue light glancing from her eyes and a circle of filigreed crystals falling about her feet. You could not say that the Spirit was smiling, only that she was the breath of joy itself. And when she spoke, such melody was in her voice that each sound articulated itself into words measured just as perfectly. The Amaranth saturated herself in the Christmas Sprit's nearness, blushing and thrilling with splendorous color. Then she said, "Every living thing grows to be like that which it loves, for every life is the fruit of its deepest desires. Now you can see how beautiful the Amaranth is."

"Because I love the Christmas Spirit," sang the flower in Vitalian's soul, and he shivered just to hear that name.

"No, it is not I alone whom she loves, but the Light whose shadow I am, the Heart of all beauty. I am only a form molded by His little hands. In me she loves Him, who alone is capable of making her blush with so much living color."

Just when the Christmas Spirit was speaking, something like a rushing wind swept through Vitalian and lifted him right off the ground. Up and away he soared, gazing upon the bright leaves and petals waving exaltedly in farewell. After him flew the Christmas Spirit, her ice earrings jingling in rounded silver tones. Their dulcet echo still was sounding within him as he entered the vaulted hollow of the Tide.

For a second, Vitalian was aware only of the infinite vastness in which he was enclosed, of the unending ebb and flow, of the motionless swaying of the Tide. There was a great tug when the Christmas Spirit entered. It left him vibrating like a plucked string, singing: "O Tide, I know our joy. I know the joy that keeps you flowing endlessly in its service. After leaving you, I came to the Christmas Spirit with a full heart. I was not afraid, and I spoke to her as I had to."

The Tide responded in soundless syllables:

> On the wings of joy she rides
> Abides in loving hearts
> She rides the happy tides
> Abides in loving hearts.

Like the memory of warm sun upon his flesh, Vitalian felt upon his exposed spirit the light of the radiant beauty next to him. He spoke again: "I was small enough to find her, and strong enough to love her."

And once more came those unspoken cadences:

Rejoice forever in this most blessed hour
When shattered is the Assailant's power
Exult! Be glad! The bonds are broken
The enemy scattered, the last work spoken.

Then it was as if the Tide, by an insensible force, had propelled both Vitalian and the Christmas Spirit through a sky layered with rich strata of velvety green and black, down in a curving arc to where lay the Old Man River. The jingling of the Christmas Spirit's earrings and her high rippling laughter blended together to drop with the dew upon the rolling sands. The sky was thoroughly ribbed with veins of dusky green. These disappeared as soon as the sun lost its hold and slipped right behind the horizon, sucking all the green light down with it.

Vitalian clung to the hand of the Christmas Spirit. Turning his head, he saw a phosphorescent golden aureole shimmering high above the northern horizon. Out of it advanced streaks of solid light, livid with every imaginable shade of color. These flowed thickly southward against the sky like glowing rivers of lava. From each of them trickled tiny prismatic traceries, and wherever they flowed, wisps of cloud melted to nothing. They melted, and the stars were uncovered. Brightly they shone, like refined gold bathed in acid, and newly polished. Their gorgeous aurulent gleam was unobscured, clear through the vivid washes of color that drenched the sky. Vitalian was so enchanted that he was unaware of alighting upon the sandy shore beside Old Man River. He was startled when the Christmas Spirit burst into song:

Awake, Old Man, Awake for the Forgotten One's sake!

Her song was the voice of a hundred silver trumpets.

Arise! Arise! And scatter your spray!

He could have led might marching armies and conquered a thousand continents:

Awake! Awake! For the Forgotten One's sake
Arise! Arise! And open your eyes
Let torrents be gay and waterspouts play
Let waterspouts quake and high waves break
Awake! Awake!

Old Man River sat bolt upright in his bed, and huge waves rolled downstream in the direction of his distant feet. Innumerable spiny fish, great and small, arched out of the water, spun about like compass needles, and plunged back dead center into the concentric circles they had made. Calciferous crabs scattered out of the churning folds of his hair and inundated the shore, making a thick carpet of waving, protruding eyes, of mean claws and pointy green-brown shells. The Old Man River was nothing but a never-ending gush of water, yet he kept his rippled shape and did not flow all away. His continuous plashing and sousing drowned out any other sound, and you breathed in his fresh briny odor until it coursed with your blood all through your body, bringing cool refreshment to every cell. Shiny black mussels and trailing tendrils of seaweed held to his trunk and shoulders, and these were here and there encrusted with great bunches of barnacles. He turned his head, swishing the water about in his eyes. When it had settled, he beheld the Christmas Spirit standing by him in the driving spray, the white gossamer gown, her arms outstretched to him. There was a roiling agitation from deep in the river; tremendous bubbles burst open upon the surface, and there rose up towering geysers that made the whole river look like one immense dancing fountain. Old Man River must have been shaking with laughter, for tumbling cataracts and drenching billows came spilling out over the banks. Vitalian and the Christmas Spirit were awash in the flood; they floated like corks on the cool water. Around and around they whirled in the funnel of a prodigious whirlpool. The Christmas Spirit's dripping hair was like melted gold.

This water drenched you like no other. It kept you so wet you thought you must have no skin, that perhaps you were made entirely of water yourself. Around they spun as whirlpools and waterspouts leapt from the river by the thousands, rioting like aqueous tornados all over the Desert of the Sands of Time. They whirled wildly in every direction, flooding the limitless wastes, soaking into every grain of sand. Wave after wave washed against the piled mounds of the Forgotten Ones. As the mounds melted away, there arose from each a shining beautifully formed figure. Their bodies glistened like unblemished mother of pearl. For an instant, they turned their shining faces toward the sky; there was a radiant smile and then a brilliant flash of light as they streaked into the sky. The split second when the waves washed away and the flawless bodies stood poised and straining upward was burned into Vitalian's memory. Never would be forget those beatific smiles, nor the ecstatic liberating ascensions—like meteors burning—into the heavens. He marked the long thing sheets of silver light that streaked the sky, followed their whole scintillating course right through the centers of the stars. Each one went through a star and disappeared into the golden glow beyond. Vitalian had seen many beautiful things on his journey, but nothing that compared with this: not even the Christmas Spirit herself.

After all the Forgotten had ascended through the stars, the whirlpool in which the two had been revolving began to unwind. It wobbled for a few seconds upon its axis, flattened out, and let them gently down into the billowy waters. The whole desert had become one vast lake, its surface rippled with circular currents. Old Man River could not be seen, for he too had become part of the lake. But by the way the water made him feel as new on the outside as the Tide did on the inside, Vitalian knew that he must still be there somewhere. And you can feel him for yourself. The next time you bathe in the sea on a summer day, you'll know what I mean.

Through the dripping strands of hair that hung before her shining eyes, the Christmas Spirit thanked him, thanked him for remembering the Forgotten Ones. Her praise thrilled him completely, and his heart leaped out to her. He thought it was this love that lifted them high above the waters. But instead, it was a great wave that had formed unnoticed beneath them. It rumbled with Old Man River's gravelly laughter and then rushed southward toward the line of trees in the distance. Upon its crest the pair tumbled happily over and over, outstripping the steady phosphorescent advance of the Northern Lights across the sky. Right through the symmetrical trunks and forked branches of the sky-touching trees they went, and out to the other side where there was no more sea. Yet still the wave held itself together and danced upon the foothills, gleefully riding over banks, boulders, and thorny bushes on its way. Up and down through the landscape it rumbled, through the fields of furze, and eventually up the side of a particularly large and familiar hill. At its summit stood an old man, huge, unbent by age, bearded, and crowned with a corona of fur.

"Beerbluff!" Vitalian cried as he and the Christmas Spirit slid down the cylindrical face of the wave. *Beerbluff Thunderbelly*, he thought when the warm copper-colored eyes focused upon him and the wave collapsed to trickle away in little rivulets among the rocks.

Next to the Christmas Spirit, who was youth itself, Beerbluff looked even more ancient and wizened than before. For a moment the dull ache of remembered pains crossed Vitalian's heart; he thought of the howling Ill Wind, the broken chimneys, and the awful cold. In fact, even now there was a moist acrid odor that dampened the air.

But there she was, the beautiful Christmas Spirit. The luxurious folds of her hair flowed like molten gold almost to her sandaled feet. She and Beerbluff said nothing to one another. They did not need to, for their correspondence lay far beyond the world of words.

Now if you had been looking down at the three from somewhere above, you would have seen an amber incandescence enveloping them: an oval bulb of brightness that illuminated the hilltop under the lightening, color-filled skies.

Suddenly the Christmas Spirit wrinkled her nose, and with a quick wave of her delicate hand sent forth a fresh breath of air. The acrid smell that Vitalian had noticed evaporated, and the fog that clung to the thorny bushes was torn up and blown away. One could hear the sound of a deep breath being drawn, as if every living thing in the valley were at once refreshing itself with draughts of pure Christmastime air.

Ribbons of bright pink and glowing green were wrapping up the sky. Farther back a solid barge of tight-fitting varicolored shafts of light inched southward, scraping the sky clean and polishing the unburied stars. There was Regulus and Rigel again, and tomboyish Bellatrix and blustering Betelgeuse. But the largest and brightest star of all was directly overhead. Its eight points were perfectly symmetrical, sharp, and tapered as the blade of a dagger. It twinkled so gaily that you thought it must have been newly created. Then with joy, Vitalian recognized it as his old friend Aldebaran, a giant so gloriously golden that he wanted to hold its richness in his hands.

Away in the East there was a yellowish-white glow, while down in the valley lights were appearing here and there in the dark window blanks of the houses. Vitalian suddenly longed with all his heart for a yellow sun, for the hot and heavy rays that draw forth salty perspiration. Meanwhile, Beerbluff and the Christmas Spirit were growing pale in the rising light. Their features were beautiful, but shone with a transparency that made Vitalian feel they were sharing their presence with some other world. He looked at them, realizing once more how much he loved them. Yes, the hot yellow sun was delicious, but what was it next to that golden glow that irresistibly drew him above the throne of the Northern Lights? And what was a warm bed, or even hot ginger cakes, compared to the exultant joy he felt when he leaped about the sky upon the rainbow bridge, or heard in his bursting heart the majestic Music of the Spheres, or felt in his soul the soundless syllables of the Tide? Vitalian knew he would come back to all these things again someday. And then there would be no parting, nor any need for the triple golden beam to be reflected upon him. No, he would rise above the Northern Lights and know the Heart directly. But not now. Now it was his lot to walk beneath this heavy yellow sun and watch the stars from far below.

"Go home now," said old Beerbluff softly. The only part of him that you could not see clear through were the copper discs of his eyes. "You have obeyed, and now you are free. You will see me no more."

The Christmas Spirit, too, was now little more than a diaphanous form draped with graceful gossamer folds of white. The ever-refreshing great blue seas of her eyes, in which Vitalian had bathed since he had known her, were almost disembodied in the pearly light.

The Northern Lights set the sky ablaze, piling himself into heaving arcs of fiery color. From the base of these arcs radiated huge beams of vermilion, like shimmering fans or ribbed seashells displayed against the sky. There were waving sheets of iridescent lilac grained with bits of dusky purples and giant shimmering aquamarine draperies fluttering with gilded edges. The village houses, the stubbled fields of furze, the ground itself were flushed rubescently with the reflection of a riot of color such as had never before been known in Deephaven.

Vitalian ached with a hollow hurt as he could barely make out the euphonious tones of the voice he had come to know: "Be gentle, Vitalian, be good. Keep pure for me and always love the unremembered ones of the world. I am the bride of simple souls, and my only abode is in loving hearts. So have your heart open for me. Have it ready so that you may someday find me again."

His hearing yearned out after the faint jingling, and his sight ached to resolve the featureless, wax-like luster that opaqued the air before him. Oh, what was wrong with this fair, green-earthed, yellow-sunned world where Beerbluff was old and the Christmas Spirit so hard to see, so impossible to touch or possess? Come back, Christmas Spirit, came back again. I love you! And Beerbluff, good Beerbluff, go in peace beyond the stars. Cradle me in your memory when you bask in that golden presence. I hope I shall not be long behind you.

And with the clean wind drying the tears in his eyes, Vitalian made his way down the hill: a small worldling figure outlined by the fluttering fires in the sky. Here and there from among the clustered houses arose a simple strain; it came as a fond souvenir of a cloudless, long-ago childhood:

> On this very day
> The Christmas Spirit is on her way
> We'll sing, dance, and play
> For the Christmas Spirit is on her way.

He passed the rough cabins of the hardy men who lived on the margins of the valley and then broke into an excited run as he entered the narrow lanes of the village. From all sides came the short claps of bolts drawn back and the clatter of chains swinging free. Doors cracked open, and many a homely human head emerged cautiously outside. In the half-light Vitalian did not leap upon flying feet as he did in the realms of gold, yet his slippers still slapped against the hard packed snow with fairy-like lightness. From the dark alleys and streets emerged scores of high-voiced puppies, whose fluffy coats of steel gray were wooly and lamb-like to the touch. They followed happily along and sped with Vitalian between the close-packed rows of houses, over piles of broken chimney bricks, and perhaps stopping just long enough for a playful tumble. Finally Vitalian turned into his own street, and just as the Northern Lights was tapering into daylight and the whitish light in the East was about to blast into dawn, he stood before the old front door he had left, it seemed, so long ago. How oaken and solid it looked! But it opened without a sound after a strong shove, and as the puppies cavorted about in the street, he stepped in upon the stone floor of his home. The fire in the hearth flared, welcoming him with a gentle pat of warmth. The bed was waiting too, turned down to invite him between the cozy covers. From the adjoining room came sighs and snores. So Vitalian crawled deep into bed and curled up. He closed his eyes.

The bed was waiting too

Before long he was shaken awake by a big hand on his shoulder. Through dreamy mists, he heard Father's deep voice: "Arise quickly, son, for the Christmas Spirit is on her way. Yes, I believe she is very near." Overnight, Father had acquired may more wrinkles about his eyes; they radiated like the spokes of a wheel.

When Vitalian turned and stretched, it was as if someone outside was pouring huge buckets of liquid sunshine right through the open window. There was a fresh scent of fir trees upon the wind, and from outdoors came the repeated strain:

> The Christmas Spirit is on her way
> She comes this very day
> Time to laugh, time for play
> The Christmas Spirit is on her way.

He leaped out of bed, and the first thing he did was run quickly to place a kiss upon Mother's ruddy cheek. She turned from the hearth where a great black pot had been hung atop the fire and held him tightly.

"The night is far too long," she said, "for then sleep takes me away from you. Where do you go? What do you do?" She held him and looked up and down. Then she turned back to the pot. "Just look at this, the Christmas Spirit is finally on her way, and Vitalian is standing before the fire with his pajamas on. Run and get dressed. Or do you think the Christmas Spirit has nothing better to do than wait for lazy little boys?"

"She is very near now," said Father, sniffing the air. His cheeks were all puffed out from trying to contain the chortling laughter that threatened to erupt from beneath his beard.

"On her way, almost here," sang the many voices outside.

Vitalian tried to get dressed. First it was the unbleached woolen sock that got stuck first on one toe and then on the other. Then it was leather boots whose polished brass buckles had each to be clasped carefully in order. And of course, the trousers just refused to be pulled on over those boots, and Vitalian had to lie back on his bed to puff and tug at them with all his might. Meanwhile he heard the jubilant voices: "Dance, dance! Sing, sing! She is very near…"

Yes, there was a happy jingle in the air. Now the men were shouting and the ladies mirthful. The dogs barked, and the children jumped about. Everyone was out in the streets. Vitalian, athrill with the coming of the Christmas Spirit, ran out too, frantically stuffing two stubborn flannel shirttails into his trousers.

The sunlight streamed out of a brilliant blue sky; the stars in it had not faded away as usual but grew brighter, etched there in all their richness. The clouds, too, were silhouetted with scintillating contours of silver, piled atop one another like fluffy mountains, reaching out to embrace the stars.

From their places, the stars chirped and twinkled, until off they broke with loud cracks and exploded into great gilded snowstars. As they drifted to earth, they sang their sidereal songs against the rich crystal tones of the unseen ice earrings. Every now and then could be heard a vibrating peal as of a deep-bowled bell: these were the golden sandals of the Christmas Spirit as she stepped upon the silver linings of the clouds. Auriga, Antares, Sirius, Spica, and the whole thick astral array followed in turn, until the earth was covered with a shining gold-dusty carpet. The last to fall from the heavens was Aldebaran, who did so in luminous solitary splendor, chiming like some huge grandfather clock.

The concert that followed his descent rivaled even the Music of the Spheres. However, its beauty was of a different kind: it was sure and direct, transparent and pure, woven solidly enough to accompany the thick tissue of life. Each modulation was a new decision reached, and every cadence another year that had passed. The contrapuntal articulation of the song was no more than the harmonic unfolding of life in Deephaven as it progressed through the years.

These melodies were heard by the ears. But eventually they too resolved into a lovely silence, a concord that was somehow suffused with a perfumed presence toward which every heart yearned. It was like the settling of conflict, the untangling of contradictions, life undisturbed by change. Then into this halcyon silence, breaking above the sheeted rooftops where the snow reflected the rays of the yellow sun, came the canorous peal of footsteps upon the clouds. Then there broke upon the earth a fierce ringing of miraculous ice earrings, frosted bracelets, and at last the linings of the clouds drew apart. From their silver folds descended the golden-haired gay Spirit of Christmas. The chaste folds of her gown fluttered like a diaphanous flag over the entire valley. Her laughter was like that of the most festive spring that had ever bubbled forth, or it was like all the Birds of Paradise chirping in unison, or the song of passion flowers in their ecstasy. Beautiful too were those sandaled feet, those hands more perfect than snow upon the untrodden heights. Her breath outdid the perfume of all the honeysuckle that ever was. With every merry shake of her head or wave of her arms, there went shivering forth a blushing arc of frosted rainbows that fell sweetly upon the earth. Joy had come to Deephaven again. You looked at her and were drawn into those cooling eyes where your soul was washed clean with deliriums of happiness.

Wherever you turned, there was the twinkling of happy eyes, far more lovely than the twinkling of the stars, and laughter that made you even forget the singing of the snowflakes. Cheeks were pinched, hands were shaken, and cold noses kissed until they were quite warm again. The folds of the Christmas Spirit's gown drifted in the refreshing wind to the far horizons, and her eyes blended with the blue of the sky as if they were passageways to heaven. The rainbows she sprinkled were deep and rich to the touch. They fell and burned through your body and into your soul, where they were like seeds blossoming into flowers of kindliness and love.

The sun perched majestically atop a throne of silver cloud. For a moment its bright disc could be seen right through the Christmas Spirit. Deep within its burning light was a Child who raised a chubby arm, and with three fingers extended traced a great sign over them.

The odor of hot food engulfed the village, and before long the tinkling of glasses mingled with the laughter. As for Vitalian, it all seemed hardly possible. Had he really crossed the Sands of Time, ascended Bifrost, and spoken to the Northern Lights? Most fantastic of all, did he dare believe that the beautiful Christmas Spirit had spoken to him?

Pangs of love shook him, and he went off alone. He was aware that Deephaven could never again be his real home. From now on he would see everything differently, would think and live differently. He could never lightly speak of, never touch, this love so deep inside. Vitalian gathered his patience together like a treasure; he would wait to see her again, beneath the throne of the Northern Lights. Day after day he would bloom were he had been planted. Yes, he resolved that his heart would be open and spotlessly pure, gentle, kind, and loving to all. The little and weary things of the world would get to know him well. Never would they come to him without a blessing, nor leave without some gift. No one would ever be forgotten in his sight.

Time went on as it does, and as year followed year, Vitalian Snowstar never forgot the promise that had been made to him: "I will never leave your heart." When it came time for him to work, he took up his ax and, like Beerbluff, grew large and happy. In old age, his hair and beard grew long and white.

He spent many a night strolling about the fields and hills outside the village, always alone except for the gray puppies whom the withering years never seemed to touch. He looked long at the stars, never tiring of their beauty. Their pale golden glow gradually faded into the silver you see today, but not before lending a permanent copper sheen to the old watcher's eyes. And every Christmas those same eyes grew happy as Vitalian recalled the days when his lovely Christmas Spirit had bodily visited the earth

She never came visibly to this world again, and eventually the people of Deephaven—busy as they were with the business of life—forgot all about her. They didn't remember that the stars were at one time made of gold, and that they used to sing and fall upon the earth in the form of great gilded snowstars.

So you may think that this old world of ours is today dull and unhappy. But this is not so. It's true, of course, that you'll only rarely see the silver lining of a cloud, and that the Christmas Spirit appears no longer amid a shower of sparkling rainbows. Yet she does come still, and you may learn to recognize her. Have you ever heard a Christmas carol and felt a surge of joy deep inside? And doesn't a heavy snowfall on Christmas Eve make you want to curl up cozily near the fire, happy just to be close to your loved ones? Well, then, the Christmas carol is an echo of the snowflake songs, and the deep comfortable joy inside is none other than the Christmas Spirit, whose ice earrings are ringing in the chambers of your soul.

You see, then, that things have not changed so terribly much. Be happy. The Christmas Spirit still visits the earth, and you may get to know her well. Just be careful to always have a place ready for her. Let kindness sweep your heart clean, so that it is empty, ready, and simple as a rough wooden manger. Then line it carefully with the straw of good deeds. If you do all this, I will make you a promise. I promise that a most loving and divine Child, heralded by the Christmas Spirit, will come to be born there. You will never know such peace. He is to be your happiness, your strength, your life, your all. And, dear children, there is only one thing I ask for myself: that when with trembling joy and expectation you gently pull aside the covers of your heart to find Him lying there, lean close to His little ear and whisper a remembrance of me.

ABOUT THE
AUTHOR

Anthony Mazzone studied literature and philosophy at LaSalle University, the University of Illinois, and the University of Fribourg. He believes there is none among earthly delights more noble than literature.

ABOUT THE
ILLUSTRATOR

Janis Mazzone studied at Temple University and has taught art at the high school level. She is the wife of the author.

The small town of Narberth, Pennsylvania is where they shelter in place.

CPSIA information can be obtained
at www.ICGtesting.com
Printed in the USA
BVHW021439221220
596261BV00001B/3